The End of the Story

by

Jack London

Rise of Douai

Copyright © 2013 Rise of Douai

ISBN-13: 978-1494793685

ISBN-10: 1494793687

About the Author

John Griffith "Jack" London (born John Griffith Chaney, January 12, 1876 – November 22, 1916) was an American author, journalist, and social activist. He was a pioneer in the then-burgeoning world of commercial magazine fiction and was one of the first fiction writers to obtain worldwide celebrity and a large fortune from his fiction alone. He is best remembered as the author of The Call of the Wild and White Fang, both set in the Klondike Gold Rush, as well as the short stories "To Build a Fire", "An Odyssey of the North", and "Love of Life". He also wrote of the South Pacific in such stories as "The Pearls of Parlay" and "The Heathen", and of the San Francisco Bay area in The Sea Wolf.

London was a passionate advocate of unionization, socialism, and the rights of workers and wrote several powerful works dealing with these topics such as his dystopian novel The Iron Heel, his non-fiction exposé The People of the Abyss, and The War of the Classes.

The End of the Story

I

The table was of hand-hewn spruce boards, and the men who played whist had frequent difficulties in drawing home their tricks across the uneven surface. Though they sat in their undershirts, the sweat noduled and oozed on their faces; yet their feet, heavily moccasined and woollen-socked, tingled with the bite of the frost. Such was the difference of temperature in the small cabin between the floor level and a yard or more above it. The sheet-iron Yukon Stove roared red-hot, yet, eight feet away, on the meat-shelf, placed low and beside the door, lay chunks of solidly frozen moose and bacon. The door, a third of the way up from the bottom, was a thick rime. In the chinking between the logs at the back of the bunks the frost showed white and glistening. A window of oiled paper furnished light. The lower portion of the paper, on the inside, was coated an inch deep with the frozen moisture of the men's breath.

They played a momentous rubber of whist, for the pair that lost was to dig a fishing hole through the seven feet of ice and snow that covered the Yukon.

"It's mighty unusual, a cold snap like this in March," remarked the man who shuffled. "What would you call it, Bob?"

"Oh, fifty-five or sixty below--all of that. What do you make it, Doc?"

4

Doc turned his head and glanced at the lower part of the door with a measuring eye.

"Not a bit worse than fifty. If anything, slightly under--say forty-nine. See the ice on the door. It's just about the fifty mark, but you'll notice the upper edge is ragged. The time she went seventy the ice climbed a full four inches higher." He picked up his hand, and without ceasing from sorting called "Come in," to a knock on the door.

The man who entered was a big, broad-shouldered Swede, though his nationality was not discernible until he had removed his ear-flapped cap and thawed away the ice which had formed on beard and moustache and which served to mask his face. While engaged in this, the men at the table played out the hand.

"I hear one doctor faller stop this camp," the Swede said inquiringly, looking anxiously from face to face, his own face haggard and drawn from severe and long endured pain. "I come long way. North fork of the Whyo."

"I'm the doctor. What's the matter?"

In response, the man held up his left hand, the second finger of which was monstrously swollen. At the same time he began a rambling, disjointed history of the coming and growth of his affliction.

"Let me look at it," the doctor broke in impatiently.

5

"Lay it on the table. There, like that."

Tenderly, as if it were a great boil, the man obeyed.

"Humph," the doctor grumbled. "A weeping sinew. And travelled a hundred miles to have it fixed. I'll fix it in a jiffy. You watch me, and next time you can do it yourself."

Without warning, squarely and at right angles, and savagely, the doctor brought the edge of his hand down on the swollen crooked finger. The man yelled with consternation and agony. It was more like the cry of a wild beast, and his face was a wild beast's as he was about to spring on the man who had perpetrated the joke.

"That's all right," the doctor placated sharply and authoritatively. "How do you feel? Better, eh? Of course. Next time you can do it yourself--Go on and deal, Strothers. I think we've got you."

Slow and ox-like, on the face of the Swede dawned relief and comprehension. The pang over, the finger felt better. The pain was gone. He examined the finger curiously, with wondering eyes, slowly crooking it back and forth. He reached into his pocket and pulled out a gold-sack.

"How much?"

The doctor shook his head impatiently. "Nothing.

I'm not practising--Your play, Bob."

The Swede moved heavily on his feet, re-examined the finger, then turned an admiring gaze on the doctor.

"You are good man. What your name?"

"Linday, Doctor Linday," Strothers answered, as if solicitous to save his opponent from further irritation.

"The day's half done," Linday said to the Swede, at the end of the hand, while he shuffled. "Better rest over to-night. It's too cold for travelling. There's a spare bunk."

He was a slender brunette of a man, lean-cheeked, thin-lipped, and strong. The smooth-shaven face was a healthy sallow. All his movements were quick and precise. He did not fumble his cards. The eyes were black, direct, and piercing, with the trick of seeming to look beneath the surfaces of things. His hands, slender, fine and nervous, appeared made for delicate work, and to the most casual eye they conveyed an impression of strength.

"Our game," he announced, drawing in the last trick. "Now for the rub and who digs the fishing hole."

A knock at the door brought a quick exclamation from him.

"Seems we just can't finish this rubber," he

7

complained, as the door opened. "What's the matter with you?"--this last to the stranger who entered.

The newcomer vainly strove to move his icebound jaws and jowls. That he had been on trail for long hours and days was patent. The skin across the cheekbones was black with repeated frost-bite. From nose to chin was a mass of solid ice perforated by the hole through which he breathed. Through this he had also spat tobacco juice, which had frozen, as it trickled, into an amber-coloured icicle, pointed like a Van Dyke beard.

He shook his head dumbly, grinned with his eyes, and drew near to the stove to thaw his mouth to speech. He assisted the process with his fingers, clawing off fragments of melting ice which rattled and sizzled on the stove.

"Nothing the matter with me," he finally announced. "But if they's a doctor in the outfit he's sure needed. They's a man up the Little Peco that's had a ruction with a panther, an' the way he's clawed is something scand'lous."

"How far up?" Doctor Linday demanded.

"A matter of a hundred miles."

"How long since?"

"I've ben three days comin' down."

8

"Bad?"

"Shoulder dislocated. Some ribs broke for sure. Right arm broke. An' clawed clean to the bone most all over but the face. We sewed up two or three bad places temporary, and tied arteries with twine."

"That settles it," Linday sneered. "Where were they?"

"Stomach."

"He's a sight by now."

"Not on your life. Washed clean with bug-killin' dope before we stitched. Only temporary anyway. Had nothin' but linen thread, but washed that, too."

"He's as good as dead," was Linday's judgment, as he angrily fingered the cards.

"Nope. That man ain't goin' to die. He knows I've come for a doctor, an' he'll make out to live until you get there. He won't let himself die. I know him."

"Christian Science and gangrene, eh?" came the sneer. "Well, I'm not practising. Nor can I see myself travelling a hundred miles at fifty below for a dead man."

"I can see you, an' for a man a long ways from dead."

9

Linday shook his head. "Sorry you had your trip for nothing. Better stop over for the night."

"Nope. We'll be pullin' out in ten minutes."

"What makes you so cocksure?" Linday demanded testily.

Then it was that Tom Daw made the speech of his life.

"Because he's just goin' on livin' till you get there, if it takes you a week to make up your mind. Besides, his wife's with him, not sheddin' a tear, or nothin', an' she's helpin' him live till you come. They think a almighty heap of each other, an' she's got a will like hisn. If he weakened, she'd just put her immortal soul into hisn an' make him live. Though he ain't weakenin' none, you can stack on that. I'll stack on it. I'll lay you three to one, in ounces, he's alive when you get there. I got a team of dawgs down the bank. You ought to allow to start in ten minutes, an' we ought to make it back in less'n three days because the trail's broke. I'm goin' down to the dawgs now, an' I'll look for you in ten minutes."

Tom Daw pulled down his earflaps, drew on his mittens, and passed out.

"Damn him!" Linday cried, glaring vindictively at the closed door.

10

II

That night, long after dark, with twenty-five miles behind them, Linday and Tom Daw went into camp. It was a simple but adequate affair: a fire built in the snow; alongside, their sleeping-furs spread in a single bed on a mat of spruce boughs; behind the bed an oblong of canvas stretched to refract the heat. Daw fed the dogs and chopped ice and firewood. Linday's cheeks burned with frost-bite as he squatted over the cooking. They ate heavily, smoked a pipe and talked while they dried their moccasins before the fire, and turned in to sleep the dead sleep of fatigue and health.

Morning found the unprecedented cold snap broken. Linday estimated the temperature at fifteen below and rising. Daw was worried. That day would see them in the canyon, he explained, and if the spring thaw set in the canyon would run open water. The walls of the canyon were hundreds to thousands of feet high. They could be climbed, but the going would be slow.

Camped well in the dark and forbidding gorge, over their pipe that evening they complained of the heat, and both agreed that the thermometer must be above zero--the first time in six months.

"Nobody ever heard tell of a panther this far north," Daw was saying. "Rocky called it a cougar. But I shot a-many of 'em down in Curry County, Oregon, where I come from, an' we called 'em panther.

11

Anyway, it was a bigger cat than ever I seen. It was sure a monster cat. Now how'd it ever stray to such out of the way huntin' range?--that's the question."

Linday made no comment. He was nodding. Propped on sticks, his moccasins steamed unheeded and unturned. The dogs, curled in furry balls, slept in the snow. The crackle of an ember accentuated the profound of silence that reigned. He awoke with a start and gazed at Daw, who nodded and returned the gaze. Both listened. From far off came a vague disturbance that increased to a vast and sombre roaring. As it neared, ever-increasing, riding the mountain tops as well as the canyon depths, bowing the forest before it, bending the meagre, crevice-rooted pines on the walls of the gorge, they knew it for what it was. A wind, strong and warm, a balmy gale, drove past them, flinging a rocket-shower of sparks from the fire. The dogs, aroused, sat on their haunches, bleak noses pointed upward, and raised the long wolf howl.

"It's the Chinook," Daw said.

"It means the river trail, I suppose?"

"Sure thing. And ten miles of it is easier than one over the tops." Daw surveyed Linday for a long, considering minute. "We've just had fifteen hours of trail," he shouted above the wind, tentatively, and again waited. "Doc," he said finally, "are you game?"

12

For answer, Linday knocked out his pipe and began to pull on his damp moccasins. Between them, and in few minutes, bending to the force of the wind, the dogs were harnessed, camp broken, and the cooking outfit and unused sleeping furs lashed on the sled. Then, through the darkness, for a night of travel, they churned out on the trail Daw had broken nearly a week before. And all through the night the Chinook roared and they urged the weary dogs and spurred their own jaded muscles. Twelve hours of it they made, and stopped for breakfast after twenty-seven hours on trail.

"An hour's sleep," said Daw, when they had wolfed pounds of straight moose-meat fried with bacon.

Two hours he let his companion sleep, afraid himself to close his eyes. He occupied himself with making marks upon the soft-surfaced, shrinking snow. Visibly it shrank. In two hours the snow level sank three inches. From every side, faintly heard and near, under the voice of the spring wind, came the trickling of hidden waters. The Little Peco, strengthened by the multitudinous streamlets, rose against the manacles of winter, riving the ice with crashings and snappings.

Daw touched Linday on the shoulder; touched him again; shook, and shook violently.

"Doc," he murmured admiringly. "You can sure go some."

The   weary   black   eyes,   under   heavy   lids,

13

acknowledged the compliment.

"But that ain't the question. Rocky is clawed something scand'lous. As I said before, I helped sew up his in'ards. Doc...." He shook the man, whose eyes had again closed. "I say, Doc! The question is: can you go some more?--hear me? I say, can you go some more?"

The weary dogs snapped and whimpered when kicked from their sleep. The going was slow, not more than two miles an hour, and the animals took every opportunity to lie down in the wet snow.

"Twenty miles of it, and we'll be through the gorge," Daw encouraged. "After that the ice can go to blazes, for we can take to the bank, and it's only ten more miles to camp. Why, Doc, we're almost there. And when you get Rocky fixed up, you can come down in a canoe in one day."

But the ice grew more uneasy under them, breaking loose from the shore-line and rising steadily inch by inch. In places where it still held to the shore, the water overran and they waded and slushed across. The Little Peco growled and muttered. Cracks and fissures were forming everywhere as they battled on for the miles that each one of which meant ten along the tops.

"Get on the sled, Doc, an' take a snooze," Daw invited.

The glare from the black eyes prevented him from

repeating the suggestion.

As early as midday they received definite warning of the beginning of the end. Cakes of ice, borne downward in the rapid current, began to thunder beneath the ice on which they stood. The dogs whimpered anxiously and yearned for the bank.

"That means open water above," Daw explained. "Pretty soon she'll jam somewheres, an' the river'll raise a hundred feet in a hundred minutes. It's us for the tops if we can find a way to climb out. Come on! Hit her up I! An' just to think, the Yukon'll stick solid for weeks."

Unusually narrow at this point, the great walls of the canyon were too precipitous to scale. Daw and Linday had to keep on; and they kept on till the disaster happened. With a loud explosion, the ice broke asunder midway under the team. The two animals in the middle of the string went into the fissure, and the grip of the current on their bodies dragged the lead-dog backward and in. Swept downstream under the ice, these three bodies began to drag to the edge the two whining dogs that remained. The men held back frantically on the sled, but were slowly drawn along with it. It was all over in the space of seconds. Daw slashed the wheel-dog's traces with his sheath-knife, and the animal whipped over the ice-edge and was gone. The ice on which they stood, broke into a large and pivoting cake that ground and splintered against the shore ice and rocks. Between them they got the sled ashore and up into a crevice in time to see the ice-cake up-edge, sink, and down-shelve from view.

Meat and sleeping furs were made into packs, and the sled was abandoned. Linday resented Daw's taking the heavier pack, but Daw had his will.

"You got to work as soon as you get there. Come on."

It was one in the afternoon when they started to climb. At eight that evening they cleared the rim and for half an hour lay where they had fallen. Then came the fire, a pot of coffee, and an enormous feed of moosemeat. But first Linday hefted the two packs, and found his own lighter by half.

"You're an iron man, Daw," he admired.

"Who? Me? Oh, pshaw! You ought to see Rocky. He's made out of platinum, an' armour plate, an' pure gold, an' all strong things. I'm mountaineer, but he plumb beats me out. Down in Curry County I used to 'most kill the boys when we run bear. So when I hooks up with Rocky on our first hunt I had a mean idea to show 'm a few. I let out the links good an' generous, 'most nigh keepin' up with the dawgs, an' along comes Rocky a-treadin' on my heels. I knowed he couldn't last that way, and I just laid down an' did my dangdest. An' there he was, at the end of another hour, a-treadin' steady an' regular on my heels. I was some huffed.

16

'Mebbe you'd like to come to the front an' show me how to travel,' I says. 'Sure,' says he. An' he done it! I stayed with 'm, but let me tell you I was plumb tuckered by the time the bear tree'd.

"They ain't no stoppin' that man. He ain't afraid of nothin'. Last fall, before the freeze-up, him an' me was headin' for camp about twilight. I was clean shot out-- ptarmigan--an' he had one cartridge left. An' the dawgs tree'd a she grizzly. Small one. Only weighed about three hundred, but you know what grizzlies is. 'Don't do it,' says I, when he ups with his rifle. 'You only got that one shot, an' it's too dark to see the sights.'

"'Climb a tree,' says he. I didn't climb no tree, but when that bear come down a-cussin' among the dawgs, an' only creased, I want to tell you I was sure hankerin' for a tree. It was some ruction. Then things come on real bad. The bear slid down a hollow against a big log. Downside, that log was four feet up an' down. Dawgs couldn't get at bear that way. Upside was steep gravel, an' the dawgs'd just naturally slide down into the bear. They was no jumpin' back, an' the bear was a-manglin' 'em fast as they come. All underbrush, gettin' pretty dark, no cartridges, nothin'.

"What's Rocky up an' do? He goes downside of log, reaches over with his knife, an' begins slashin'. But he can only reach bear's rump, an' dawgs bein' ruined fast, one-two-three time. Rocky gets desperate. He don't like to lose his dawgs. He jumps on top log, grabs bear by the slack of the rump, an' heaves over back'ard right

17

over top of that log. Down they go, kit an' kaboodle, twenty feet, bear, dawgs, an' Rocky, slidin', cussin', an' scratchin', ker-plump into ten feet of water in the bed of stream. They all swum out different ways. Nope, he didn't get the bear, but he saved the dawgs. That's Rocky. They's no stoppin' him when his mind's set."

It was at the next camp that Linday heard how Rocky had come to be injured.

"I'd ben up the draw, about a mile from the cabin, lookin' for a piece of birch likely enough for an axe-handle. Comin' back I heard the darndest goings-on where we had a bear trap set. Some trapper had left the trap in an old cache an' Rocky'd fixed it up. But the goings-on. It was Rocky an' his brother Harry. First I'd hear one yell and laugh, an' then the other, like it was some game. An' what do you think the fool game was? I've saw some pretty nervy cusses down in Curry County, but they beat all. They'd got a whoppin' big panther in the trap an' was takin' turns rappin' it on the nose with a light stick. But that wa'n't the point. I just come out of the brush in time to see Harry rap it. Then he chops six inches off the stick an' passes it to Rocky. You see, that stick was growin' shorter all the time. It ain't as easy as you think. The panther'd slack back an' hunch down an' spit, an' it was mighty lively in duckin' the stick. An' you never knowed when it'd jump. It was caught by the hind leg, which curious, too, an' it had some slack I'm tellin' you.

"It was just a game of dare they was playin', an' the

stick gettin' shorter an' shorter an' the panther madder 'n madder. Bimeby they wa'n't no stick left--only a nubbin, about four inches long, an' it was Rocky's turn. 'Better quit now,' says Harry. 'What for?' says Rocky. 'Because if you rap him again they won't be no stick left for me,' Harry answers. 'Then you'll quit an' I win,' says Rocky with a laugh, an' goes to it.

"An' I don't want to see anything like it again. That cat'd bunched back an' down till it had all of six feet slack in its body. An' Rocky's stick four inches long. The cat got him. You couldn't see one from t'other. No chance to shoot. It was Harry, in the end, that got his knife into the panther's jugular."

"If I'd known how he got it I'd never have come," was Linday's comment.

Daw nodded concurrence.

"That's what she said. She told me sure not to whisper how it happened."

"Is he crazy?" Linday demanded in his wrath.

"They're all crazy. Him an' his brother are all the time devilin' each other to tom-fool things. I seen them swim the riffle last fall, bad water an' mush-ice runnin'--on a dare. They ain't nothin' they won't tackle. An' she's 'most as bad. Not afraid some herself. She'll do anything Rocky'll let her. But he's almighty careful with her. Treats her like a queen. No camp-work or

19

such for her. That's why another man an' me are hired on good wages. They've got slathers of money an' they're sure dippy on each other. 'Looks like good huntin',' says Rocky, when they struck that section last fall. 'Let's make a camp then,' says Harry. An' me all the time thinkin' they was lookin' for gold. Ain't ben a prospect pan washed the whole winter."

Linday's anger mounted. "I haven't any patience with fools. For two cents I'd turn back."

"No you wouldn't," Daw assured him confidently. "They ain't enough grub to turn back, an' we'll be there to-morrow. Just got to cross that last divide an' drop down to the cabin. An' they's a better reason. You're too far from home, an' I just naturally wouldn't let you turn back."

Exhausted as Linday was, the flash in his black eyes warned Daw that he had overreached himself. His hand went out.

"My mistake, Doc. Forget it. I reckon I'm gettin' some cranky what of losin' them dawgs."

III

Not one day, but three days later, the two men, after being snowed in on the summit by a spring blizzard, staggered up to a cabin that stood in a fat bottom beside the roaring Little Peco. Coming in from the bright sunshine to the dark cabin, Linday observed

20

little of its occupants. He was no more than aware of two men and a woman. But he was not interested in them. He went directly to the bunk where lay the injured man. The latter was lying on his back, with eyes closed, and Linday noted the slender stencilling of the brows and the kinky silkiness of the brown hair. Thin and wan, the face seemed too small for the muscular neck, yet the delicate features, despite their waste, were firmly moulded.

"What dressings have you been using?" Linday asked of the woman.

"Corrosive, sublimate, regular solution," came the answer.

He glanced quickly at her, shot an even quicker glance at the face of the injured man, and stood erect. She breathed sharply, abruptly biting off the respiration with an effort of will. Linday turned to the men.

"You clear out--chop wood or something. Clear out."

One of them demurred.

"This is a serious case," Linday went on. "I want to talk to his wife."

"I'm his brother," said the other.

21

To him the woman looked, praying him with her eyes. He nodded reluctantly and turned toward the door.

"Me, too?" Daw queried from the bench where he had flung himself down.

"You, too."

Linday busied himself with a superficial examination of the patient while the cabin was emptying.

"So?" he said. "So that's your Rex Strang."

She dropped her eyes to the man in the bunk as if to reassure herself of his identity, and then in silence returned Linday's gaze.

"Why don't you speak?"

She shrugged her shoulders. "What is the use? You know it is Rex Strang."

"Thank you. Though I might remind you that it is the first time I have ever seen him. Sit down." He waved her to a stool, himself taking the bench. "I'm really about all in, you know. There's no turnpike from the Yukon here."

He drew a penknife and began extracting a thorn from his thumb.

22

"What are you going to do?" she asked, after a minute's wait.

"Eat and rest up before I start back."

"What are you going to do about...." She inclined her head toward the unconscious man.

"Nothing."

She went over to the bunk and rested her fingers lightly on the tight-curled hair.

"You mean you will kill him," she said slowly. "Kill him by doing nothing, for you can save him if you will."

"Take it that way." He considered a moment, and stated his thought with a harsh little laugh. "From time immemorial in this weary old world it has been a not uncommon custom so to dispose of wife-stealers."

"You are unfair, Grant," she answered gently. "You forget that I was willing and that I desired. I was a free agent. Rex never stole me. It was you who lost me. I went with him, willing and eager, with song on my lips. As well accuse me of stealing him. We went together."

"A good way of looking at it," Linday conceded. "I see you are as keen a thinker as ever, Madge. That must have bothered him."

"A keen thinker can be a good lover--"

"And not so foolish," he broke in.

"Then you admit the wisdom of my course?"

He threw up his hands. "That's the devil of it, talking with clever women. A man always forgets and traps himself. I wouldn't wonder if you won him with a syllogism."

Her reply was the hint of a smile in her straight-looking blue eyes and a seeming emanation of sex pride from all the physical being of her.

"No, I take that back, Madge. If you'd been a numbskull you'd have won him, or any one else, on your looks, and form, and carriage. I ought to know. I've been through that particular mill, and, the devil take me, I'm not through it yet."

His speech was quick and nervous and irritable, as it always was, and, as she knew, it was always candid. She took her cue from his last remark.
"Do you remember Lake Geneva?"

"I ought to. I was rather absurdly happy."

She nodded, and her eyes were luminous. "There is such a thing as old sake. Won't you, Grant, please, just remember back ... a little ... oh, so little ... of what we were to each other ... then?"

"Now you're taking advantage," he smiled, and returned to the attack on his thumb. He drew the thorn out, inspected it critically, then concluded. "No, thank you. I'm not playing the Good Samaritan."

"Yet you made this hard journey for an unknown man," she urged.

His impatience was sharply manifest. "Do you fancy I'd have moved a step had I known he was my wife's lover?"

"But you are here ... now. And there he lies. What are you going to do?"

"Nothing. Why should I? I am not at the man's service. He pilfered me."

She was about to speak, when a knock came on the door.

"Get out!" he shouted.

"If you want any assistance--"

"Get out! Get a bucket of water! Set it down outside!"

"You are going to...?" she began tremulously.

"Wash up."

25

She recoiled from the brutality, and her lips tightened.

"Listen, Grant," she said steadily. "I shall tell his brother. I know the Strang breed. If you can forget old sake, so can I. If you don't do something, he'll kill you. Why, even Tom Daw would if I asked."

"You should know me better than to threaten," he reproved gravely, then added, with a sneer: "Besides, I don't see how killing me will help your Rex Strang."

She gave a low gasp, closed her lips tightly, and watched his quick eyes take note of the trembling that had beset her.

"It's not hysteria, Grant," she cried hastily and anxiously, with clicking teeth. "You never saw me with hysteria. I've never had it. I don't know what it is, but I'll control it. I am merely beside myself. It's partly anger--with you. And it's apprehension and fear. I don't want to lose him. I do love him, Grant. He is my king, my lover. And I have sat here beside him so many dreadful days now. Oh, Grant, please, please."

"Just nerves," he commented drily. "Stay with it. You can best it. If you were a man I'd say take a smoke."

She went unsteadily back to the stool, where she watched him and fought for control. From the rough fireplace came the singing of a cricket. Outside two

26

wolf-dogs bickered. The injured man's chest rose and fell perceptibly under the fur robes. She saw a smile, not altogether pleasant, form on Linday's lips.

"How much do you love him?" he asked.

Her breast filled and rose, and her eyes shone with a light unashamed and proud. He nodded in token that he was answered.

"Do you mind if I take a little time?" He stopped, casting about for the way to begin. "I remember reading a story--Herbert Shaw wrote it, I think. I want to tell you about it. There was a woman, young and beautiful; a man magnificent, a lover of beauty and a wanderer. I don't know how much like your Rex Strang he was, but I fancy a sort of resemblance. Well, this man was a painter, a bohemian, a vagabond. He kissed--oh, several times and for several weeks--and rode away. She possessed for him what I thought you possessed for me ... at Lake Geneva. In ten years she wept the beauty out of her face. Some women turn yellow, you know, when grief upsets their natural juices.

"Now it happened that the man went blind, and ten years afterward, led as a child by the hand, he stumbled back to her. There was nothing left. He could no longer paint. And she was very happy, and glad he could not see her face. Remember, he worshipped beauty. And he continued to hold her in his arms and believe in her beauty. The memory of it was vivid in

27

him. He never ceased to talk about it, and to lament that he could not behold it.

"One day he told her of five great pictures he wished to paint. If only his sight could be restored to paint them, he could write finis and be content. And then, no matter how, there came into her hands an elixir. Anointed on his eyes, the sight would surely and fully return."

Linday shrugged his shoulders.

"You see her struggle. With sight, he could paint his five pictures. Also, he would leave her. Beauty was his religion. It was impossible that he could abide her ruined face. Five days she struggled. Then she anointed his eyes."

Linday broke off and searched her with his eyes, the high lights focused sharply in the brilliant black.

"The question is, do you love Rex Strang as much as that?"
"And if I do?" she countered.

"Do you?"

"Yes."

"You can sacrifice? You can give him up?"

Slow and reluctant was her "Yes."

"And you will come with me?"

"Yes." This time her voice was a whisper. "When he is well--yes."

"You understand. It must be Lake Geneva over again. You will be my wife."

She seemed to shrink and droop, but her head nodded.

"Very well." He stood up briskly, went to his pack, and began unstrapping. "I shall need help. Bring his brother in. Bring them all in. Boiling water--let there be lots of it. I've brought bandages, but let me see what you have in that line.--Here, Daw, build up that fire and start boiling all the water you can.--Here you," to the other man, "get that table out and under the window there. Clean it; scrub it; scald it. Clean, man, clean, as you never cleaned a thing before. You, Mrs. Strang, will be my helper. No sheets, I suppose. Well, we'll manage somehow.--You're his brother, sir. I'll give the anaesthetic, but you must keep it going afterward. Now listen, while I instruct you. In the first place--but before that, can you take a pulse?..."

IV

Noted for his daring and success as a surgeon, through the days and weeks that followed Linday exceeded himself in daring and success. Never,

29

because of the frightful mangling and breakage, and because of the long delay, had he encountered so terrible a case. But he had never had a healthier specimen of human wreck to work upon. Even then he would have failed, had it not been for the patient's catlike vitality and almost uncanny physical and mental grip on life.

There were days of high temperature and delirium; days of heart-sinking when Strang's pulse was barely perceptible; days when he lay conscious, eyes weary and drawn, the sweat of pain on his face. Linday was indefatigable, cruelly efficient, audacious and fortunate, daring hazard after hazard and winning. He was not content to make the man live. He devoted himself to the intricate and perilous problem of making him whole and strong again.

"He will be a cripple?" Madge queried.

"He will not merely walk and talk and be a limping caricature of his former self," Linday told her. "He shall run and leap, swim riffles, ride bears, fight panthers, and do all things to the top of his fool desire. And, I warn you, he will fascinate women just as of old. Will you like that? Are you content? Remember, you will not be with him."

"Go on, go on," she breathed. "Make him whole. Make him what he was."

More than once, whenever Strang's recuperation

permitted, Linday put him under the anaesthetic and did terrible things, cutting and sewing, rewiring and connecting up the disrupted organism. Later, developed a hitch in the left arm. Strang could lift it so far, and no farther. Linday applied himself to the problem. It was a case of more wires, shrunken, twisted, disconnected. Again it was cut and switch and ease and disentangle. And all that saved Strang was his tremendous vitality and the health of his flesh.

"You will kill him," his brother complained. "Let him be. For God's sake let him be. A live and crippled man is better than a whole and dead one."

Linday flamed in wrath. "You get out! Out of this cabin with you till you can come back and say that I make him live. Pull--by God, man, you've got to pull with me with all your soul. Your brother's travelling a hairline razor-edge. Do you understand? A thought can topple him off. Now get out, and come back sweet and wholesome, convinced beyond all absoluteness that he will live and be what he was before you and he played the fool together. Get out, I say."

The brother, with clenched hands and threatening eyes, looked to Madge for counsel.

"Go, go, please," she begged. "He is right. I know he is right."

Another time, when Strang's condition seemed more promising, the brother said:

"Doc, you're a wonder, and all this time I've forgotten to ask your name."

"None of your damn business. Don't bother me. Get out."

The mangled right arm ceased from its healing, burst open again in a frightful wound.

"Necrosis," said Linday.

"That does settle it," groaned the brother.

"Shut up!" Linday snarled. "Get out! Take Daw with you. Take Bill, too. Get rabbits--alive--healthy ones. Trap them. Trap everywhere."

"How many?" the brother asked.

"Forty of them--four thousand--forty thousand--all you can get. You'll help me, Mrs. Strang. I'm going to dig into that arm and size up the damage. Get out, you fellows. You for the rabbits."

And he dug in, swiftly, unerringly, scraping away disintegrating bone, ascertaining the extent of the active decay.

"It never would have happened," he told Madge, "if he hadn't had so many other things needing vitality first. Even he didn't have vitality enough to go around. I was watching it, but I had to wait and chance it. That piece must go. He could manage without it, but rabbit-bone will make it what it was."

From the hundreds of rabbits brought in, he weeded out, rejected, selected, tested, selected and tested again, until he made his final choice. He used the last of his chloroform and achieved the bone-graft-
-living bone to living bone, living man and living rabbit immovable and indissolubly bandaged and bound together, their mutual processes uniting and reconstructing a perfect arm.

And through the whole trying period, especially as Strang mended, occurred passages of talk between Linday and Madge. Nor was he kind, nor she rebellious.

"It's a nuisance," he told her. "But the law is the law, and you'll need a divorce before we can marry again. What do you say? Shall we go to Lake Geneva?"

"As you will," she said.

And he, another time: "What the deuce did you see in him anyway? I know he had money. But you and I were managing to get along with some sort of comfort. My practice was averaging around forty thousand a year then--I went over the books afterward. Palaces and steam yachts were about all that was denied you."

"Perhaps you've explained it," she answered. "Perhaps you were too interested in your practice.

Maybe you forgot me."

"Humph," he sneered. "And may not your Rex be too interested in panthers and short sticks?"

He continually girded her to explain what he chose to call her infatuation for the other man.

"There is no explanation," she replied. And, finally, she retorted, "No one can explain love, I least of all. I only knew love, the divine and irrefragable fact, that is all. There was once, at Fort Vancouver, a baron of the Hudson Bay Company who chided the resident Church of England parson. The dominie had written home to England complaining that the Company folk, from the head factor down, were addicted to Indian wives. 'Why didn't you explain the extenuating circumstances?' demanded the baron. Replied the dominie: 'A cow's tail grows downward. I do not attempt to explain why the cow's tail grows downward. I merely cite the fact.'"

"Damn clever women!" cried Linday, his eyes flashing his irritation.

"What brought you, of all places, into the Klondike?" she asked once.

"Too much money. No wife to spend it. Wanted a rest. Possibly overwork. I tried Colorado, but their telegrams followed me, and some of them did themselves. I went on to Seattle. Same thing. Ransom ran his wife out to me in a special train. There was no escaping it. Operation successful. Local newspapers got wind of it. You can imagine the rest. I had to hide, so I ran away to Klondike. And--well, Tom Daw found me playing whist in a cabin down on the Yukon."

Came the day when Strang's bed was carried out of doors and into the sunshine.

"Let me tell him now," she said to Linday.

"No; wait," he answered.

Later, Strang was able to sit up on the edge of the bed, able to walk his first giddy steps, supported on either side.

"Let me tell him now," she said.

"No. I'm making a complete job of this. I want no set-backs. There's a slight hitch still in that left arm. It's a little thing, but I am going to remake him as God made him. Tomorrow I've planned to get into that arm and take out the kink. It will mean a couple of days on his back. I'm sorry there's no more chloroform. He'll just have to bite his teeth on a spike and hang on. He can do it. He's got grit for a dozen men."

Summer came on. The snow disappeared, save on the far peaks of the Rockies to the east. The days lengthened till there was no darkness, the sun dipping at midnight, due north, for a few minutes beneath the horizon. Linday never let up on Strang. He studied his walk, his body movements, stripped him again and again and for the thousandth time made him flex all his muscles. Massage was given him without end, until Linday declared that Tom Daw, Bill, and the brother were properly qualified for Turkish bath and osteopathic hospital attendants. But Linday was not yet satisfied. He put Strang through his whole repertoire of physical feats, searching him the while for hidden weaknesses. He put him on his back again for a week, opened up his leg, played a deft trick or two with the smaller veins, scraped a spot of bone no larger than a coffee grain till naught but a surface of healthy pink remained to be sewed over with the living flesh.

"Let me tell him," Madge begged.

"Not yet," was the answer. "You will tell him only when I am ready."

July passed, and August neared its end, when he ordered Strang out on trail to get a moose. Linday kept at his heels, watching him, studying him. He was slender, a cat in the strength of his muscles, and he walked as Linday had seen no man walk, effortlessly, with all his body, seeming to lift the legs with supple muscles clear to the shoulders. But it was without heaviness, so easy that it invested him with a peculiar grace, so easy that to the eye the speed was deceptive. It was the killing pace of which Tom Daw had complained. Linday toiled behind, sweating and

36

panting; from time to time, when the ground favoured, making short runs to keep up. At the end of ten miles he called a halt and threw himself down on the moss.

"Enough!" he cried. "I can't keep up with you."

He mopped his heated face, and Strang sat down on a spruce log, smiling at the doctor, and, with the camaraderie of a pantheist, at all the landscape.

"Any twinges, or hurts, or aches, or hints of aches?" Linday demanded.

Strang shook his curly head and stretched his lithe body, living and joying in every fibre of it.

"You'll do, Strang. For a winter or two you may expect to feel the cold and damp in the old wounds. But that will pass, and perhaps you may escape it altogether."

"God, Doctor, you have performed miracles with me. I don't know how to thank you. I don't even know your name."

"Which doesn't matter. I've pulled you through, and that's the main thing."

"But it's a name men must know out in the world," Strang persisted. "I'll wager I'd recognise it if I heard it."

"I think you would," was Linday's answer. "But it's beside the matter. I want one final test, and then I'm done with you. Over the divide at the head of this creek is a tributary of the Big Windy. Daw tells me that last year you went over, down to the middle fork, and back again, in three days. He said you nearly killed him, too. You are to wait here and camp to-night. I'll send Daw along with the camp outfit. Then it's up to you to go to the middle fork and back in the same time as last year."

V

"Now," Linday said to Madge. "You have an hour in which to pack. I'll go and get the canoe ready. Bill's bringing in the moose and won't get back till dark. We'll make my cabin to-day, and in a week we'll be in Dawson."

"I was in hope...." She broke off proudly.
"That I'd forego the fee?"

"Oh, a compact is a compact, but you needn't have been so hateful in the collecting. You have not been fair. You have sent him away for three days, and robbed me of my last words to him."

"Leave a letter."

"I shall tell him all."

"Anything less than all would be unfair to the three of us," was Linday's answer.

When he returned from the canoe, her outfit was packed, the letter written.

"Let me read it," he said, "if you don't mind."

Her hesitation was momentary, then she passed it over.

"Pretty straight," he said, when he had finished it. "Now, are you ready?"

He carried her pack down to the bank, and, kneeling, steadied the canoe with one hand while he extended the other to help her in. He watched her closely, but without a tremor she held out her hand to his and prepared to step on board.

"Wait," he said. "One moment. You remember the story I told you of the elixir. I failed to tell you the end. And when she had anointed his eyes and was about to depart, it chanced she saw in the mirror that her beauty had been restored to her. And he opened his eyes, and cried out with joy at the sight of her beauty, and folded her in his arms."

She waited, tense but controlled, for him to continue, a dawn of wonder faintly beginning to show in her face and eyes.

"You are very beautiful, Madge." He paused, then added drily, "The rest is obvious. I fancy Rex Strang's arms won't remain long empty. Good-bye."

"Grant...." she said, almost whispered, and in her voice was all the speech that needs not words for understanding.

He gave a nasty little laugh. "I just wanted to show you I wasn't such a bad sort. Coals of fire, you know."

"Grant...."

He stepped into the canoe and put out a slender, nervous hand.

"Good-bye," he said.

She folded both her own hands about his.

"Dear, strong hand," she murmured, and bent and kissed it.

He jerked it away, thrust the canoe out from the bank, dipped the paddle in the swift rush of the current, and entered the head of the riffle where the water poured glassily ere it burst into a white madness of foam.

THE END

RISE OF DOUAI

RISE OF DOUAI

TWITTER : @RISEOFDOUAI

- AN IDIOT'S GUIDE TO: BEE
  HUNTING BY JOHN LOCKARD,
  EDITED BY ARSALAN AHMED
  (2012)(PAPERBACK) ISBN-10:
  1478383550

- THE RISE OF DOUAI BY
  ARSALAN AHMED
  (2012)(PAPERBACK) ISBN-10:
  1479267783

- THE RICHEST MAN IN BABYLON
  BY GEORGE S. CLASON (2012)
  (PAPERBACK) ISBN-10: 1479377341

- THINK AND GROW RICH BY
  NAPOLEON HILL (2012)
  (PAPERBACK) ISBN-10: 1480061638

- AS A MAN THINKETH BY MR
  JAMES ALLEN (2012)
  (PAPERBACK) ISBN-10: 1480088161
- HOW TO ANALYZE PEOPLE ON

SIGHT BY ELSIE BENEDICT (PAPERBACK) ISBN-10: 1480081272

- THE ART OF WAR BY MR SUN TZU (PAPERBACK) ISBN-10: 1480082007
- MACBETH BY MR WILLIAM SHAKESPEARE (PAPERBACK) ISBN-10: 1480060682
- A CHRISTMAS CAROL BY MR CHARLES DICKENS ISBN-10: 1481194755
- CREATING CAPITAL: MONEY-MAKING AS AN AIM IN BUSINESS BY MR FREDRICK L LIPMAN ISBN-10: 1481158996
- GETTING GOLD: A PRACTICAL TREATISE FOR PROSPECTORS, MINERS, AND STUDENTS BY MR JOSEPH COLIN FRANCIS JOHNSON ISBN-10: 1481090984
- THE INTERPRETATION OF DREAMS BY MR SIGMUND FREUD ISBN-10: 1481134558
- THE COMMUNIST MANIFESTO BY MR KARL MARX AND MR FRIDRICK ENGLES ISBN-10:

1480112445

- THE PRINCE BY MR NICCOLO MACHIAVELLI ISBN-10: 1480119601
- THE WAY TO WEALTH BY MR BENJAMIN FRANKLIN ISBN-10: 1480099651
- THE ART OF MONEY GETTING - OR GOLDEN RULES FOR MAKING MONEY (SUCCESS PRINCIPLES) BY MR PHINEAS TAYLOR BARNUM ISBN-10: 1480138622

Twitter : @RiseofDouai

Made in the USA
Las Vegas, NV
13 December 2022

62008560R00026